AWES

BY MICHAEL CHABON

OME MAN:

The MYSTERY INTRUDER

Quill Tree Books
An Imprint of HarperCollinsPublishers

ILLUSTRATED *BY* JAKE PARKER

Hey, what's up?

It's me, Awesome Man, the super-intense superdude. And this is Moskowitz the Awesome Dog.

I fight bad guys,

and help people,

and try to fix stuff.

Also, I try not to smash too many buildings, which can be hard sometimes, like for example when you're fighting a giant Plutonian octolizard.

Everyone in Awesome City knows I'm the greatest superhero in town.

Tickle

Okay, to be honest, I'm also the only superhero in town. Just me and Moskowitz. And that's the way we like it.

HOORAY FOR AWESOME MAN

But have you heard the news? There's a new
superhero coming to Awesome City! And I
don't think that sounds very awesome—at all.

I wonder what kind of powers this new superhero is going to have. Like, maybe he'll be called Steel Tornado.

He'll be able to spin around hyperfast and drill through anything, even a diamond as big as Mount Everest. He might even be able to drill a hole into the future!

Or if it's a she, maybe she'll be called Glue Girl and be able to make things stick together, no matter what. Like if an airplane is going to crash, she could glue it to a cloud.

Or maybe she'll know how to glue earthquakes back together.

Or maybe the new superhero is going to be made in a secret lab, by mad scientists, out of hot lava.

But you want to know what I wonder most of all? It's something kind of scary. So scary I better whisper it.

What if the people of Awesome City like the new superhero *more* than they like Awesome Man?

What if they decide to have a Thank You for Being Awesome Parade, but it's not for me?

What if they forget my birthday?

To be honest? Right now I don't really feel like fighting bad guys, or helping people, or fixing stuff. I'm just hanging around the Fortress of Awesome, feeling kind of blue.

Hey! The Danger Map is lighting up! There's trouble at the Awesome City Zoo!

The Flaming Eyeball is on a rampage. . . . This definitely looks like a job for Awesome Man!

But I don't move a muscle. Let the new guy handle it. Let Glue Girl, or Squid Lad, or Monkey Butt, or whoever, try to save Awesome City. Maybe then people around here will appreciate me a little more.

Maybe then they won't forget my birthday.

Moskowitz brings me a thermovulcanized protein-delivery orb. I can tell she thinks I'm being kind of a baby about the new superhero.

Okay, fine, Moskowitz.

I power up and head for the Awesome City Zoo.

I put an Awesome Power Grip on the Flaming Eyeball and douse him with some positronic rays.

The polar bears seem to think that's pretty cool. (Get it?)

But when I get back to the Fortress of Awesome,
Sister Sinister is there waiting for me! It's a trap!

No— Sister Sinister wants to call a truce! She says we have a bigger problem than each other right now. And then in her most sinister voice she says, *"He's here."*

So we go into the Fortress of Awesome
to meet the new superhero.

Can I tell you something? I am not impressed by this guy. He's bald. He's tiny. And he can't do *anything*!

You want to know what his powers
turn out to be? Let me put it this way:
Sister Sinister calls him the Screamer.
But I just call him Captain Stinky.

At night when it's time for Captain Stinky to go to bed, my secret-identity mom lets me help her get him ready. He's so tiny he has to take a bath in the sink! I guess being ultra-tiny is a *kind* of superpower.

After Captain Stinky has his bedtime snack, my secret-identity mom gives him to Sister Sinister and shows her how to pat him gently on the back. Sister Sinister finds out that Captain Stinky has two more superpowers: Supersonic Burp and Slime Blast.

Maybe the new kid is going to be okay!

Someday very soon, my secret-identity mom says, Captain Stinky is going to want to follow you everywhere.

He'll want to do
everything you do.
And he'll want you to
teach him everything
you know.

And the thing he's going to want
most, in the whole wide world, is
to be just as awesome as you.

When my secret-identity mom says that, I have to laugh. She wants to know what's so funny.

I thought I was only getting a sibling, I tell her. I didn't know I was getting a *sidekick*!

She turns off the lamp, and I lean down to give Captain Stinky a kiss. I notice maybe he's not really that stinky after all. Actually? Right now he smells kind of nice. I lower my voice to an ultra-soft hyperwhisper that only he and Moskowitz can hear.

And I say, Good night, Awesome Boy.

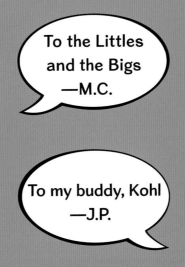

To the Littles
and the Bigs
—M.C.

To my buddy, Kohl
—J.P.

Quill Tree Books is an imprint of HarperCollins Publishers

Awesome Man: The Mystery Intruder
For information address HarperCollins Children's Books, a division of
HarperCollins Publishers, 195 Broadway, New York, NY 10007.
www.harpercollinschildrens.com

ISBN 978-0-06-287509-9

20 21 22 23 24 SCP 10 9 8 7 6 5 4 3 2 1
❖
First Edition